Christmas with Little Women

Louisa May Alcott

Illustrated by Russ Flint

Ideals Publishing
Nashville, Tennessee

ISBN 0-8249-8150-2

"Christmas won't be Christmas without any presents," grumbled Jo, lying on the rug.

"It's so dreadful to be poor!" sighed Meg, looking down at her old dress.

"We've got Father and Mother and each other," said Beth contentedly from her corner.

The four young faces on which the firelight shone brightened at the cheerful words.

"The reason Mother proposed not having any presents this Christmas was because it is going to be a hard winter for everyone," Meg said. "She thinks we ought not to spend money for pleasure. We can't do much, but we can make our little sacrifices, and ought to do it gladly. But I am afraid I don't." And Meg shook her head, as she thought regretfully of all the pretty things she wanted.

"Mother didn't say anything about our money, and she won't wish us to give up everything. Let's each buy what we want and have a little fun. I'm sure we work hard enough to earn it," cried Jo.

As young readers like to know "how people look," we will take this moment to give them a little sketch of the four sisters, who sat knitting away in the twilight, while the December snow fell quietly without, and the fire crackled cheerfully within.

Meg, the oldest of the four, was sixteen, and very pretty, with large eyes, plenty of soft, brown hair, a sweet mouth, and white hands, of which she was rather vain.

Fifteen-year-old Jo was very tall and thin, and reminded one of a colt, for she never seemed to know what to do with her long limbs. She had a decided mouth, a comical nose, and sharp, gray eyes, which appeared to see everything, and were by turns fierce, funny, or thoughtful. Her long, thick hair was her one beauty, but it was usually bundled into a net, to be out of her way. Jo had round shoulders, big hands and feet, a flyaway look to her clothes, and the uncomfortable appearance of a girl who was rapidly shooting up into a woman.

Elizabeth—or Beth, as everyone called her—was a rosy, smooth-haired, bright-eyed girl of thirteen, with a shy manner, a timid voice, and a peaceful expression which was seldom disturbed. Her father called her "Little Tranquility," and the name suited her excellently.

Amy, though the youngest, was a most important person—in her own opinion at least. A regular snow maiden, with blue eyes, and yellow hair curling on her shoulders, pale and slender, and always carrying herself like a young lady mindful of her manners.

The clock struck six and, having swept up the hearth, Beth put a pair of slippers down to warm. Somehow the sight of the old shoes had a good effect upon the girls, for Mother was coming, and everyone brightened to welcome her home. Meg stopped lecturing and lighted the lamp, Amy got out of the easy chair without being asked, and Jo forgot how tired she was as she sat up to hold the slippers nearer to the blaze.

"They are quite worn out. Marmee must have a new pair."

"I'll tell you what we'll do," said Beth, "let's each get something for Marmee for Christmas, and not get anything for ourselves."

"That's like you, dear! What will we get?" exclaimed Jo.

Everyone thought soberly for a minute, then Meg announced, "I shall give her a nice pair of gloves."

"Army shoes, the very best to be had," cried Jo.

"Some handkerchiefs, all hemmed," said Beth.

"I'll get a little bottle of cologne. She likes it, and it won't cost much, so I'll have some left to buy my pencils," added Amy.

"Let Marmee think we are getting things for ourselves, and then surprise her. We must go shopping tomorrow afternoon, Meg," said Jo, marching up and down, with her hands behind her back and her nose in the air.

"Glad to find you so merry, my girls," said a cheery voice at the door, and the girls turned to welcome a tall, motherly lady with a "can-I-help-you" look about her which was truly delightful. She was not elegantly dressed, but the girls thought the gray cloak and unfashionable bonnet covered the most splendid mother in the world.

"Well, dearies, how have you got on today? Has anyone called, Beth? How is your cold, Meg? Jo, you look tired to death. Come and kiss me, baby."

While making these maternal inquiries Mrs. March got her wet things off, her warm slippers on, and sitting down in the easy chair, drew Amy to her lap, preparing to enjoy the happiest hour of her busy day.

As they gathered about the table, Mrs. March said, with a particularly happy face, "I've got a treat for you after supper."

A quick, bright smile went round like a streak of sunshine. Beth clapped her hands, regardless of the biscuit she held, and Jo tossed up her napkin, crying, "A letter! A letter! Three cheers for Father!"

"Yes, a nice long letter. He is well, and thinks he shall get through the cold season better than we feared. He sends all sorts of loving wishes for Christmas, and an especial message to you girls," said Mrs. March, patting her pocket as if she had got a treasure there.

"I think it was so splendid of Father to go in as a chaplain when he was too old to be drafted, and not strong enough for a soldier," said Meg warmly.

"When will he come home, Marmee?" asked Beth, with a little quiver in her voice.

"Not for many months, dear, unless he is sick. He will stay and do his work faithfully as long as he can, and we won't ask for him back a minute sooner than he can be spared. Now come and hear the letter."

Their father's letter was a cheerful, hopeful letter, full of lively descriptions of camp life, marches, and military news. At the end he wrote:

"Give my girls all my dear love and a kiss. Tell them I think of them by day, pray for them by night, and find my best comfort in their affection at all times. I know they will be loving children to you, will do their duty faithfully, fight their bosom enemies bravely, and conquer themselves so beautifully that when I come back to them I may be fonder and prouder than ever of my little women."

Everybody sniffed when they came to that part; Jo wasn't ashamed of the great tear that dropped off the end of her nose. Amy didn't mind the rumpling of her curls as she hid her face on her mother's shoulder and sobbed out, "I am a selfish girl! But I'll truly try to be better, so he won't be disappointed in me by-and-by."

"We all will!" cried Meg. "I think too much of my looks and hate to work, but I won't any more, if I can help it."

"I'll try and be what he loves to call me, 'a little woman,' and not be rough and wild. I'll do my duty here instead of wanting to be somewhere else," said Jo.

Beth said nothing, but wiped away her tears with the blue sock she was knitting while she resolved in her quiet little soul to be all that Father hoped to find when the year brought his happy homecoming.

At nine they stopped work, and sang, as usual, before they went to bed. No one but Beth could get much music out of the old piano, but she had a way of softly touching the yellow keys and making a pleasant accompaniment to the simple songs they sang.

Jo was the first to wake in the gray dawn of Christmas morning. No stockings hung at the fireplace, and for a moment she felt disappointed. Then she slipped her hand under her pillow and drew out a crimson-covered Bible.

She woke Meg with a "Merry Christmas," and bade her see what was under her pillow. A green-covered Bible appeared, with a few words written by their mother, which made their one present very precious in their eyes. Presently Beth and Amy woke to rummage and find their little books also—one dove-colored, the other blue—and all sat looking at and talking about their little books, while the east grew rosy with the coming day.

"Girls," said Meg seriously, looking from the tumbled head beside her to the two little nightcapped ones in the room beyond, "Mother wants us to read and love and mind these books, and we must begin at once. You can do as you please, but I shall keep my book on the table here and read a little every morning as soon as I wake, for I know it will do me good and help me through the day."

"How good Meg is! Come, Amy, let's do as they do. I'll help you with the hard words, and they'll explain things if we don't understand," whispered Beth, very much impressed by the pretty books and her sisters' example.

The rooms were very still while the pages were softly turned, and the winter sunshine crept in to touch the bright heads and serious faces with a Christmas greeting.

"Where is Mother?" asked Meg, as she and Jo ran down to thank her for their gifts, half an hour later.

"Goodness only knows. Some poor creeter come a-beggin', and your ma went straight off to see what was needed. There never was such a woman for givin' away vittles and drink, clothes and firin'," replied Hannah, who had lived with the family since Meg was born, and was considered by them all more as a friend than a maid.

"She will be back soon, I think, so fry your cakes, and have everything ready," said Meg, looking over the presents which were collected in a basket and kept under the sofa, ready to be produced at the proper time.

"Why, where is Amy's bottle of cologne?" she added, as the flask did not appear.

"She took it out a minute ago, and went off with it to put a ribbon on it, or some such notion," replied Jo, dancing about the room to take the first stiffness off the new slippers.

"How nice my handkerchiefs look, don't they? Hannah washed and ironed them for me, and I marked them all myself," said Beth, looking proudly at the somewhat uneven letters which had cost her such labor.

"There's Mother. Hide the basket, quick!" cried Jo, as a door slammed and footsteps sounded in the hall.

Amy came in hastily, and looked rather abashed when she saw her sisters all waiting for her.

"Where have you been, and what are you hiding behind you?" asked Meg, surprised to see, by her hood and cloak, that lazy Amy had been out so early.

"Don't laugh at me, Jo! I didn't mean anyone should know till the time came. I only meant to change the little bottle for a big one, and I gave all my money to get it, and I'm truly trying not to be selfish any more."

As she spoke, Amy showed the handsome flask which replaced the cheap one, and looked so earnest and humble in her little effort to forget herself that Meg hugged her on the spot. Jo pronounced her "a trump," while Beth ran to the window, and picked her finest rose to ornament the stately bottle.

"You see, I felt ashamed of my present, after reading and talking about being good this morning, so I ran round the corner and changed it the minute I was up; and I'm so glad, for mine is the handsomest now."

Another bang of the street door sent the basket under the sofa, and the girls to the table, eager for breakfast.

"Merry Christmas, Marmee! Many of them! Thank you for our books; we read some, and mean to every day," they cried, in chorus.

"Merry Christmas, little daughters! I'm glad you began at once and hope you will keep on. But I want to say one word before we sit down. Not far away from here lies a poor woman with a little newborn baby. Six children are huddled into one bed to keep from freezing, for they have no fire. There is nothing to eat over there, and the oldest boy came to tell me they were suffering hunger and cold. My girls, will you give them your breakfast as a Christmas present?"

They were all unusually hungry, having waited nearly an hour, and for a minute no one spoke—only a minute, for Jo exclaimed impetuously, "I'm so glad you came before we began!"

"May I go and help carry the things to the poor little children?" asked Beth eagerly.

"I shall take the cream and the muffins," added Amy, heroically giving up the articles she most liked.

Meg was already covering the buck-wheats, and piling the bread onto one big plate.

"I thought you'd do it," said Mrs. March, smiling as if satisfied. "You shall all go and help me, and when we come back we will have bread and milk for breakfast, and make it up at dinnertime."

They were soon ready, and the procession set out. Fortunately it was early, and they went through back streets, so few people saw them, and no one laughed at the queer party.

A poor, bare, miserable room it was, with broken windows, no fire, ragged bedclothes, a sick mother, wailing baby, and a group of pale, hungry children cuddled under one old quilt, trying to keep warm.

How the big eyes stared and the blue lips smiled as the girls went in!

"It is good angels come to us!" said the poor woman, crying for joy.

"Funny angels in hoods and mittens," said Jo, and set them laughing.

In a few minutes it really did seem as if kind spirits had been at work there. Hannah, who had carried wood, made a fire, and stopped up the broken panes with old hats and her own

cloak. Mrs. March gave the mother tea and gruel, and comforted her with promises of help, while she dressed the little baby as tenderly as if it had been her own. The girls, meantime, spread the table, set the children round the fire, and fed them like so many hungry birds—laughing and talking.

That was a very happy breakfast, though they didn't get any of it. When they went away, leaving comfort behind, I think there were not in all the city four merrier people than the hungry little girls who gave away their breakfasts and contented themselves with bread and milk on Christmas morning.

"That's loving our neighbor better than ourselves, and I like it," said Meg, as they set out their presents while their mother was upstairs.

Not a very splendid show, but there was a great deal of love done up in the few little bundles. The tall vase of red roses, white chrysanthemums, and trailing vines, which stood in the middle, gave quite an elegant air to the table.

"She's coming! Strike up, Beth! Open the door, Amy! Three cheers for Marmee!" cried Jo, prancing about while Meg went to conduct Mother to the seat of honor. Beth played her gayest march, Amy threw open the door, and Meg acted escort with great dignity. Mrs. March was both surprised and touched, and smiled with her eyes full as she examined her presents and read the little notes which accompanied them. The slippers went on at once, a new handkerchief was slipped into her pocket, well scented with Amy's cologne, a rose from Beth was fastened in her belt, and the gloves were pronounced a "perfect fit."

There was a good deal of laughing and kissing and explaining in the simple, loving fashion which makes these holidays so pleasant at the time and so sweet to remember long afterward.

A few happy hours later, Hannah appeared, with "Mrs. March's compliments, and would the ladies walk down to supper."

This was a surprise. When the girls saw the table, they looked at one another in rapturous amazement. It was like Marmee to get up a little treat for them, but anything so fine as this was unheard of. There was ice cream—actually two dishes of it, pink and white—and cake and fruit and distracting French bonbons and, in the middle of the table, four great bouquets of hothouse flowers!

It quite took their breath away; and they stared first at the table and then at their mother, who looked as if she enjoyed it immensely.

"Is it fairies?" asked Amy.

"It's Santa Claus," said Beth.

"Mother did it." And Meg smiled her sweetest.

"All wrong. Old Mr. Laurence sent it," replied Mrs. March.

"The Laurence boy's grandfather! What in the world put such a thing into his head? We don't know him!" exclaimed Meg.

"Hannah told one of his servants about your breakfast party. He is an odd old gentleman, but that pleased him. He knew my father years ago, and he sent me a polite note this afternoon, saying he hoped I would allow him to express his friendly feeling toward my children by sending them a few trifles in honor of the day. I could not refuse, and so you have a little feast at night to make up for the bread-and-milk breakfast."

"What a special Christmas this has turned out to be!" exclaimed Meg, smelling her flowers.

"Merry Christmas, girls," said Mrs. March, with her arms open wide to embrace her little women.

"Merry Christmas, Marmee!" they cried in unison.

ABOUT THE AUTHOR

Born in 1832, Louisa May Alcott grew up in Massachusetts with her parents and three sisters. She drew upon her memories of her family and childhood in writing *Little Women*, which was published in 1868, and has since become an American classic.

Other works followed such as *Little Men* and *Eight Cousins*, but none achieved the same level of success as *Little Women*. After spending much of her last decade of life involved in the temperance and women's suffrage movements, Louisa May Alcott died in 1888.

ABOUT THE ILLUSTRATOR

Russ Flint is a well-known children's book illustrator whose works have included children's versions of such classics as Dickens' *A Christmas Carol* and *Swan Lake*. He began illustrating for children's books seven years ago and is currently involved in writing as well as illustrating children's stories.

Russ's interest in this career stemmed from a time when he would make up stories and draw pictures for his own four children. He is currently living with his family in the mountains of California, where he has a home and studio.